The Lonely Pony

Do you love ponies? Be a Pony Pal!

PONY PALS

The Lonely Pony

Jeanne Betancourt

illustrated by Susy Boyer Rigby

SCHOLASTIC INC.
New York Toronto London Auckland Sydney
Mexico City New Delhi Hong Kong

ISBN 0-439-06491-0

Text copyright ©1999 by Jeanne Betancourt.
Cover and text illustrations copyright ©1999 by Scholastic Australia. All rights reserved. Published by Scholastic Inc., 555 Broadway, New York, NY 10012, by arrangement with Scholastic Australia Pty Limited.

12 11 10 9 8 7 6 5 4 3 2 1   0 1 2 3 4 5 6/0

Printed in Australia

First Scholastic printing, February 2000
Cover and text illustrations by Susy Boyer Rigby
Typeset in Bookman

Contents

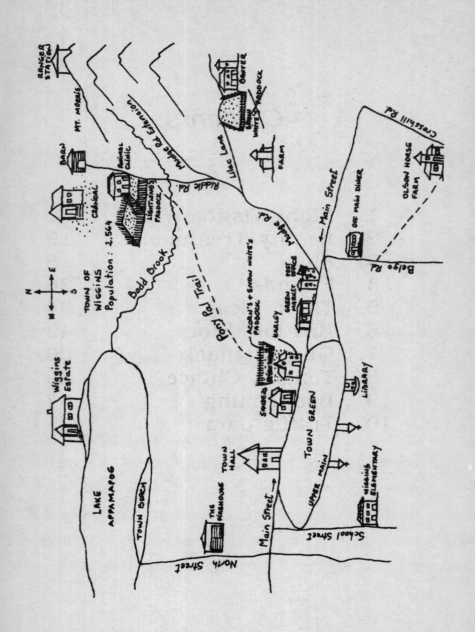

Night Visitor

A pony's angry whinny woke up Lulu Sanders. She jumped out of bed and ran to the window. Lulu looked out behind Anna Harley's house. There were usually only two ponies to be seen— Snow White and Anna's Shetland pony, Acorn. But this early morning there were *three*—two ponies in the paddock and one on the other side of the fence.

Lulu recognized the extra pony right away. It was Mimi Kline's small Shetland pony, Tongo. How did Tongo get here? Lulu wondered.

Acorn and Tongo happily sniffed noses over the fence. Snow White stood alone in the middle of the paddock. Snow White doesn't like having surprise visitors, thought Lulu.

Lulu pulled on her jeans, ran down the stairs and out the back door. By the time she reached the paddock, Anna was there, too.

"Tongo must have jumped his fence to come over here," said Anna.

"And crossed Main Street," added Lulu. "That's dangerous."

Acorn ran up to the girls. Tongo followed him. Snow White stayed in the middle of the paddock.

Lulu went over to Snow White and rubbed her neck. "It's all right, Snow White," she told her pony. "It's just Tongo."

"We'd better tell the Klines that Tongo is here," said Anna. "Mimi will be upset when she wakes up and he's not there."

Anna put Tongo in the paddock with the other ponies. Then Lulu and Anna went across

2

Main Street to the Klines' house. Mrs. Bell, the Klines' babysitter, answered the door.

"Mimi isn't up yet," Mrs. Bell told Anna and Lulu. "And Mr. and Mrs. Kline are out of town on business."

"Sorry to come so early," said Lulu.

"Tongo is at our house," explained Anna.

"He must have run away during the night," added Lulu.

"Oh, dear!" exclaimed Mrs. Bell. "How did he get out?"

"He jumped the fence," said Lulu.

"I'm surprised he can jump that high," said Anna.

"Why would he leave his own yard?" asked Mrs. Bell.

Lulu explained that ponies get lonely and like to be with other animals. "Tongo's smart," added Anna. "He found Acorn and Snow White."

Five-year-old Mimi Kline came running down

3

the stairs. "Anna! Lulu!" she shouted. "Am I going to have a riding lesson?"

"That's not why we're here," Lulu told Mimi.

Anna explained to Mimi about Tongo running away.

"He could have got hit by a car!" shrieked Mimi. "I want to get him. He's my pony."

Anna and Lulu exchanged a smile. Mimi was cute and spoiled. Just like Tongo. And both were lots of fun.

A few minutes later Mimi and Mrs. Bell went over to the Harley paddock to get Tongo. Anna put on his halter and Mimi clipped on the lead rope.

"We're going home," Mimi told her pony. "Don't run away again."

Tongo pulled away from Mimi. He didn't want to leave Acorn.

"Maybe Tongo could just stay here today," suggested Mrs. Bell.

Snow White snorted angrily at Tongo.

4

"I think Snow White's jealous," said Anna. "She doesn't want to share Acorn."

"Snow White is not jealous," Lulu told Anna. "Tongo probably did something to her that we didn't see."

"Maybe," said Anna. "Anyway, Tongo has to go home, Mimi."

"Can Acorn come to our house?" asked Mimi. "Can he play with Tongo? Please, Anna, please?"

"It might be a good idea," said Mrs. Bell.

Anna agreed. A few minutes later Anna and Acorn left with Mimi, Tongo and Mrs. Bell.

After they left, Lulu fed Snow White. Snow White ate only half of her grain and seemed sad. She already misses Acorn, thought Lulu.

Lulu looked up and saw Anna running towards her across the paddock.

"Mrs. Bell has asked me to help babysit with Mimi and Acorn all day," Anna announced. "She's really worried that Tongo will run away again."

"But we were supposed to go on a trail ride today," protested Lulu.

"This is more important," said Anna. "Tongo ran away."

Lulu knew that Anna was right.

"You can come over to the Klines', too," Anna suggested. "Rosalie Lacey is going to be there. We can both take care of the girls and Tongo."

Lulu thought for a second. She didn't feel like spending a day with the two younger girls and the spoiled pony. But most of all, she didn't want to leave Snow White alone.

"No, thanks," she said. "I'm going to go on a trail ride with Snow White."

After Anna left, Lulu went into her grandmother's beauty parlor. Grandmother Sanders was cutting a young woman's hair.

"I'm going for a trail ride," Lulu told her grandmother.

"With Anna?" Grandmother asked.

"Anna's busy," replied Lulu. "She can't go."

7

"So it's just you and your other Pony Pal, Pam," said Grandmother.

Lulu shook her head. "Pam and Lightning went to a jumping clinic for two days. It's just me and Snow White."

Grandmother stopped cutting the woman's hair and turned to Lulu. "You may not go trail riding alone, Lucinda," she said.

"But—" Lulu began.

"I won't have you riding off into the woods alone," said her grandmother.

"I won't be alone," protested Lulu. "I'll be with Snow White."

"You and Snow White may not go riding alone," Grandmother Sanders said more firmly.

"I don't have anything to do," murmured Lulu.

"You could use a hair cut," her grandmother said. "And you can give yourself a manicure. I have some pretty new nail polishes you can try."

8

"No, thanks," said Lulu. "I'm going back outside."

Lulu left the beauty parlor. She hated that she couldn't go for a trail ride alone. She took an apple from the fruit bowl in the kitchen and went out to Snow White.

When Lulu reached the fence, she held out the apple to her pony. "Come and get it," she called to Snow White.

Snow White walked slowly towards Lulu. She sniffed the apple, but didn't eat it.

"What's wrong, Snow White?" asked Lulu. "You always like apples."

Finally, Snow White took the apple in her mouth and chewed it slowly.

"You miss Acorn and Lightning," said Lulu. And I miss Anna and Pam, she thought. Life in Wiggins is boring without my Pony Pals.

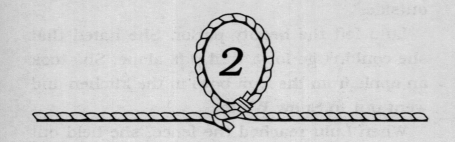

Beauty Treatment

Lulu was so bored that she let her grandmother cut her hair. While Grandmother

moved to Grandmother Sanders' house in Wiggins.

The first week that Lulu was in Wiggins she met Anna and Pam. Grandmother Sanders didn't like ponies, but Lulu's new friends did.

Pam Crandal knew a lot about ponies and horses. Her mother was a riding teacher and her father was a veterinarian. Pam had owned a pony for as long as she could remember. Anna didn't have her own pony until she was ten. Before that, Anna took riding lessons from Mrs. Crandal.

The three Pony Pals loved the outdoors and animals of all kinds. But they especially loved ponies. Pam and Lulu read loads of books about horses. But Anna didn't like to read that much. She was dyslexic, so reading was difficult for her. Instead, Anna drew and painted beautiful pictures of ponies and horses. Lulu thought Anna was a terrific artist.

"Your hair looks very pretty like this," Grandmother said.

Lulu looked at her reflection in the mirror. Her hair was shorter and a little wavy. It did look pretty. But I'd rather be on a trail ride, she thought.

"Now why don't you give yourself a nice manicure," suggested Grandmother Sanders.

"I'm going to check on Snow White," Lulu told her grandmother.

Lulu found Snow White standing near the shed, sleeping. While Snow White takes her nap, thought Lulu, I'll go and see what Anna's doing.

Lulu went across Main Street and the town green to the Klines' backyard. Anna was busily brushing Tongo, while Mimi braided his mane. Six-year-old Rosalie Lacey was there grooming Acorn. They all seemed to be having a great time.

"Hi," Anna called to Lulu. "Your hair looks great."

"Thanks," said Lulu.

"I'm making Tongo's hair pretty," said Mimi.

12

"He's going to have a sleepover with Acorn. They're best friends."

"Is Acorn staying here tonight?" Lulu asked Anna.

Anna nodded.

"But Acorn and Snow White are stablemates," protested Lulu.

"Mrs. Bell is afraid Tongo will run away again," explained Anna. "I said I'd stay over, too."

"The Klines have to figure out how to keep Tongo in his own yard," said Lulu.

"And we have to help them," said Anna.

Rosalie came over to Anna and Lulu. "Acorn's all groomed," she said excitedly. "Anna, you said I could ride."

"Me, too," said Mimi.

"Want to help?" Anna asked Lulu.

Lulu thought about Snow White . . . alone in the paddock across the street. "No, thanks," she said. "I'm going back home."

Lulu spent the rest of the day with Snow

White. She cleaned out the shed and groomed her pony. But Snow White didn't nuzzle Lulu's shoulder the way she usually did. And she didn't want any more apples.

That night Lulu had a nightmare about Snow White running away. The nightmare woke her up. She went to the bathroom window and looked out at the moonlit paddock. She couldn't see Snow White anywhere.

Lulu quickly ran down the stairs and out to the paddock. What if Snow White really had run away, she thought? How will I find her all by myself?

As Lulu passed through the gate she saw something move in the shed. It was Snow White. She ran to the shed and threw her arms around her pony's neck. "I'm so glad you're safe," she told Snow White.

It was a cold night, but Snow White's neck was hot. Lulu felt her pony's forehead. That was hot, too.

"Are you sick, Snow White?" Lulu asked.

Snow White didn't look up. Lulu noticed that Snow White's nose was running. Lulu felt scared and worried. Snow White was sick. Lulu looked at her watch. It was four o'clock in the morning. I'll call Dr. Crandal at seven o'clock, she thought. By then the Crandals would be up.

Lulu went back to the house to get her jacket, a blanket, a flashlight and a notebook. I'll write down Snow White's symptoms, she thought. And I'd better leave Grandmother a note so she doesn't think I've run away.

Lulu wrote a note to her grandmother and left it on the kitchen table.

Dear Grandmother:
I am in the shed with Snow White.
She is sick so I can't leave her alone.
Love,
Lulu

Lulu ran back out to the shed. "Don't worry, Snow White," she said. "You're not alone."

Snow White sneezed. Lulu noticed that her

16

pony was shivering. She put a lightweight horse blanket over the pony. Then, Lulu sat on the cover of the feed bin and wrapped her own blanket around her shoulders. She turned on the flashlight, opened her notebook and wrote:

SNOW WHITE IS SICK.
THIS IS WHAT IS WRONG.
Fever (I think)
Runny nose
Sneezing
Noisy breathing
Shivering
Not hungry, even for treats
Sleeping a lot

When Lulu finished the list she read it over. There are so many things wrong with Snow White, she thought sadly. I don't know how to make her better.

She checked her watch again. It was five o'clock. In two hours she'd call Dr. Crandal. She certainly needed his help.

Alone

At seven o'clock Lulu went back to the house. Her grandmother wasn't up yet, and the note was still on the kitchen table.

Lulu dialed the Crandals' phone number. Dr. Crandal answered.

"It's Lulu Sanders," Lulu told him. "Snow White is sick."

Dr. Crandal asked Lulu what was wrong. Lulu told him all of her pony's symptoms.

"Sounds like she has a respiratory infection,"

said Dr. Crandal. "I'll come over later this morning and have a look."

"Thank you," said Lulu.

"What about Acorn?" asked Dr. Crandal. "Does he have any of those symptoms?"

Lulu told Dr. Crandal that Acorn was at the Klines'. "He's been there since yesterday morning," she added.

"Good," said Dr. Crandal. "Let him stay there. We don't want Acorn to catch something from Snow White. I'll see you in about two hours. Meanwhile, keep an eye on her."

Lulu thanked Dr. Crandal again and said goodbye. She was eating a bowl of cereal when her grandmother came downstairs. "You're up early," Grandmother Sanders said.

Lulu told her grandmother about Snow White being sick.

"Poor pony," said Grandmother Sanders. She put an arm around Lulu and gave her a little hug. "Poor Lulu. You must be worried."

Lulu felt tears come into her eyes. She *was*

worried. And she was glad that her grandmother understood.

After Lulu checked on Snow White, she ran over to the Klines'. She needed to tell Anna that Acorn shouldn't come home.

Lulu knocked on the Klines' front door. Mrs. Bell answered.

"Is Anna here?" asked Lulu.

"She took Mimi to the diner for breakfast," Mrs. Bell told Lulu. "They just left. Why don't you go, too?"

Lulu explained that Snow White was sick, so she couldn't. "I'm going to see if Tongo and Acorn are sick," Lulu told Mrs. Bell.

Lulu went around to the backyard. Tongo and Acorn were standing together near the fence. She went over to them and touched their sides. Neither of them was hot. And they didn't have runny noses.

"You guys are okay," Lulu said. "Snow White's the only one that's sick."

Lulu told Mrs. Bell that Acorn and Tongo

weren't sick. "But tell Anna that Acorn should stay here," added Lulu.

Lulu waited in the shed for Dr. Crandal's visit.

The first thing Dr. Crandal did was take Snow White's temperature.

"She has a fever," Dr. Crandal told Lulu.

Next, he listened to Snow White's lungs with his stethoscope. "And she's congested," he said.

"Can she breathe all right?" asked Lulu.

"She'll be able to breathe better after I give her some medicine," explained Dr. Crandal. "Now let's see if she has a cough."

Dr. Crandal squeezed Snow White's windpipe, and she coughed.

"That sounds awful," said Lulu.

"She definitely has a respiratory infection," Dr. Crandal said.

Dr. Crandal gave Snow White cough syrup and a shot of antibiotics. Then he took a bottle of pills out of his doctor's bag. He handed them to Lulu. "These are sulfur pills," he explained.

"Crush five of them up in her food. She might like a warm mash."

"I'll give it to her right away," Lulu told him.

Dr. Crandal gave Lulu some more directions.

Lulu wrote down everything that he told her. The whole time Snow White stood quietly, with her head hanging.

Dr. Crandal put a hand on Snow White's head.

"Is she going to be okay?" Lulu asked fearfully.

"I think so," he told her. "But call me if she gets worse. And keep her away from other ponies. This is probably very contagious."

Lulu thanked Dr. Crandal. "Are Pam and Lightning still coming home tomorrow?" she asked.

"As far as I know," answered Dr. Crandal.

"I hope so," said Lulu. "I miss them."

After Dr. Crandal left, Lulu looked over the list of what she had to do for Snow White.

LIST FOR CARING FOR SNOW WHITE.
Light blanket
Warm mash
5 Sulfur pills 2 times daily (crushed)
Cough syrup 2 times daily
Watch carefully

Mrs. Bell must have told Anna that Snow White is sick, thought Lulu. Why doesn't Anna come over? Doesn't she care about Snow White anymore? Doesn't she care about her Pony Pals?

Snow White coughed. Lulu ran over to her. "Dr. Crandal gave you cough medicine," she told the pony. "You're not supposed to have it again until tonight. Please get better, Snow White. Please." Lulu made Snow White a warm mash and mixed in the sulfur pill.

"Okay, Snow White," said Lulu. "Here's something delicious and good for you."

Snow White didn't even sniff the mash. She turned around and walked to the other end of the shed. Lulu followed her. "Come on, Snow White," she said. "You have to eat it." Lulu hand fed the mash to Snow White until she was sure she'd eaten all of the sulfur pills.

Lulu wished with all her heart that her Pony Pals were there to help her. Will Snow White get better? She wondered. Will she get sicker?

It was lonely being an only Pony Pal. And it was scary.

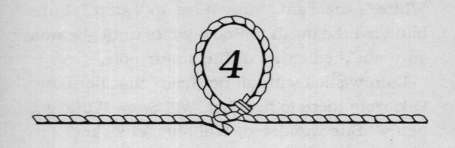

Friends?

After lunch, Lulu rubbed Snow White down
with a dry cloth. I told Mrs. Bell that Snow
White was sick five hours ago, thought Lulu.
Why hasn't Anna come over?

"Hi," said a voice behind her.

Lulu turned around. It was Anna.

"Mrs. Bell told me that Snow White's sick,"
Anna said. "How is she?"

"She feels awful," said Lulu.

Anna went to Snow White and looked into

her eyes. "Poor, Snow White," she said. "What's wrong?"

"She has a respiratory infection," explained Lulu. "It's very contagious."

Anna took a few steps away from Snow White.

"Humans can't catch it," added Lulu. "Just other ponies."

Lulu told Anna all about Dr. Crandal's visit. Then she told her about the quarantine. "So Acorn can't come home while Snow White's sick," concluded Lulu.

"Good," said Anna. "It will give us time to solve the Tongo problem. We have to figure out how to keep him in his own yard."

Lulu put down the rubbing cloth and stared at Anna. She couldn't believe her ears. "How can you say it's good that Snow White is sick?" she asked.

"I didn't say it's good that Snow White's sick!" exclaimed Anna. "I said it's good that Acorn is with Tongo. So Tongo won't run away again. We have time to solve the Tongo problem."

"The Klines should just get another pony," Lulu told Anna. "Then Tongo can have his own stablemate."

"They said no more ponies," Anna told Lulu. "This is a big Pony Pal Problem."

Snow White being sick is the big Pony Pal Problem, thought Lulu.

"You have to come up with an idea for Tongo," insisted Anna. "Pam, too, as soon as she comes home."

"I don't have time to worry about Tongo," Lulu told Anna in an angry voice. "I have to take care of Snow White."

Mimi and Rosalie were running across the Harleys' backyard towards the paddock.

"Anna! Anna!" shouted Rosalie.

"We were looking for you," yelled Mimi.

Snow White was startled by the loud voices and jumped back.

"Keep them away from Snow White," Lulu warned Anna. "She's supposed to rest."

28

"I'll take them back to Mimi's," said Anna. "We'll talk about our Pony Pal Problem later."

Anna turned and ran to meet Mimi and Rosalie.

Lulu watched Anna and the two younger girls leave. They laughed as they raced one another up the driveway. Anna isn't even worried about Snow White, Lulu thought. I'd be worried if Acorn was sick. Or Lightning.

Lulu spent the rest of the afternoon with Snow White. After dinner she gave her another warm mash with pills. This time Snow White ate all of the mash right away.

That night Lulu took her sleeping bag and flashlight out to the shed. "I'll be your stablemate tonight," she told Snow White.

Lulu woke up in the middle of the night. It was dark, but Lulu could still see her white pony standing in the corner of the shed. Lulu slipped out of her sleeping bag and went over to Snow White. She felt her neck.

29

"You don't feel so hot anymore," Lulu whispered to Snow White.

Next, Lulu checked to see if her pony's nose was running. It wasn't.

Lulu brushed the forelock off Snow White's forehead. The pony opened her eyes and looked at Lulu. Snow White nickered and nuzzled her head into Lulu's shoulder.

Lulu wrapped her arm over Snow White's neck. "I think you're getting better," she said.

Lulu went back to her sleeping bag and they both went back to sleep.

The next morning Lulu fed Snow White and cleaned out the shed. Snow White seemed livelier. Lulu was laying out fresh straw when she saw Pam running towards her. Dr. Crandal was right behind her. Lulu ran to meet them.

"How's Snow White?" was the first thing Pam said.

"I think she's better," said Lulu. "I slept out here with her last night."

"I just got home and Dad told me," said Pam. "I came right away." Pam looked around. "Where's Anna?"

"She's at the Klines'," said Lulu. "She's there all the time now. Babysitting and pony-sitting. Acorn's there, too. I'll tell you all about it later."

The girls watched silently as Dr. Crandal checked Snow White's temperature, her lungs and nostrils.

"She's much better," Dr. Crandal told them. "By tomorrow she'll be a hundred percent." He smiled at Lulu. "You did a great job taking care of her. Continue the sulfur pills for a week."

"What about the cough syrup?" asked Lulu.

"Continue with it as long as she's still coughing," he said.

Out of the corner of her eye, Lulu saw Anna running towards them. Lulu didn't bother to wave to her.

"Hi, everybody," said Anna when she reached them. "How's Snow White? She looks better. Is he cured?"

"She," corrected Lulu. "Snow White is a she, you called her he."

"Sorry," said Anna softly. "I just made a mistake."

Lulu knew that she'd hurt Anna's feelings, but she didn't care. Why should she when Anna didn't even care about Snow White?

"My dad said Snow White is better," Pam told Anna.

"But she still shouldn't be with other ponies," added Dr. Crandal. "Can Acorn stay at the Klines' one more night?"

"Sure," said Anna. "Tongo's been lonely."

"Tomorrow, Tongo and Acorn can come over here with Snow White," suggested Dr. Crandal.

"That won't work," Anna explained. "Snow White doesn't like Tongo. She gets jealous."

"Snow White is *not* jealous," Lulu practically shouted at Anna.

Lulu glared at Anna. Didn't Anna understand anything about ponies? Didn't she love Snow White anymore?

Three Ideas

Dr. Crandal snapped his veterinarian bag closed. "Pam, we have to get back," he said. He gave Snow White a final pat and turned to leave.

Pam looked from Lulu to Anna. "What's going on?" she asked in a quiet voice. "How come you guys are fighting?"

"We're not fighting," said Anna. "Lulu's just upset because Snow White was sick."

"You don't even care about Snow White anymore," Lulu told Anna. "All you think about is lonely Tongo. Well, Snow White is lonely, too. And she was really sick."

"I love Snow White," protested Anna. "And I want Acorn to come home. But we have to be sure Tongo won't run away again."

"Pam, let's go," Dr. Crandal called from the other end of the paddock.

"I have to go," Pam told Lulu and Anna. "I have to help my mom with her lessons this afternoon. But let's have a Pony Pal Meeting at the diner tonight. Okay?"

"The Klines are coming home this afternoon," said Anna. "So I can do it."

"I can, too," said Lulu. "If Snow White doesn't get sick again."

"Six o'clock at the diner," suggested Pam.

"We should have ideas for how to keep Tongo home," said Anna. "It's a Pony Pal Problem."

"Good idea," agreed Pam.

Pam turned and ran to catch up with her father.

Anna and Lulu just looked at each other. Lulu still felt angry with Anna.

"What are you doing this afternoon?" Anna asked Lulu.

"Staying with Snow White," said Lulu.

"I told Mrs. Bell I'd take Mimi to the library," said Anna. "Then we have to clean out the shed and groom the ponies."

"So, see you," said Lulu.

"Yeah," said Anna. "See you."

Anna left and Lulu was alone again.

Lulu wished with all her heart that things would go back to normal. But she knew they wouldn't until the Tongo problem was solved. And until she stopped being angry with Anna.

Lulu walked into Off-Main Diner at six o'clock. Anna's mother owned the diner. It was a favorite meeting place for the Pony Pals. Pam and Anna were already in the Pony Pals' favorite booth.

Lulu went over and sat next to Pam.

"How's Snow White?" asked Anna.

"She's okay," answered Lulu.

"Let's put in our orders and start the meeting," suggested Pam.

While the girls waited for their food, they talked about the Tongo problem.

"Here's my idea," said Pam. She handed Lulu a piece of paper and Lulu read it out loud.

The Klines should make their fence higher. That way Tongo can't run away.

"That's a good idea," said Lulu.

"The Klines own a hardware store," said Pam. "So it won't cost them too much money."

"I hope they don't mind having a bigger fence," said Lulu.

"And there's still the problem of Tongo being lonely," added Pam.

"That's what my idea is about," said Anna. She took out a drawing and put it on the table.

"Tongo needs a stablemate," explained Anna. "Mimi's parents said no more ponies. So I think we should try animals that are smaller, like a duck."

"I thought the kitten they adopted would be a stablemate for Tongo," said Pam.

"Chicago is more a people cat," explained Anna. "He stays inside at night."

"Which is when Tongo gets lonely," Lulu pointed out.

"What if we pick out a stablemate for Tongo and he doesn't like it?" asked Pam.

"Or the animal doesn't like Tongo," added Anna.

"That's what my idea is about," said Lulu. She handed her idea to Pam to read out loud.

Find a stablemate for Tongo at
St. Francis Animal Shelter.

"There are loads of animals at St. Francis that need a home," said Lulu. "We could try out different ones, until we find the one that Tongo likes."

"Excellent!" exclaimed Pam.

"The animal has to like Tongo, too," Anna reminded them. "Tongo acts bratty sometimes. I bet Tongo did something to make Snow White angry. You know, the night he came to our paddock."

"That's what *I* think happened, too," agreed Lulu.

Anna smiled at Lulu. And Lulu smiled back. At least one Pony Pal Problem was solved. Lulu didn't feel so angry with Anna anymore.

"So we have three good ideas," said Lulu. "But what if the Klines don't like them?"

"That's our next problem," said Pam.

"Three Pony Pal burrito specials on deck," shouted the cook.

The Pony Pals stood up and went to get their food.

We're working together to solve the Tongo problem, thought Lulu. We have good ideas. But will the Klines want to build a new fence and adopt another animal?

Bedtime Story

After the Pony Pals ate their burritos and cleared the table, they walked over to the Klines' house.

Mrs. Kline answered the front door. She invited the three girls in and they followed her to the living room. Mr. Kline and Mimi were sitting on the couch.

"Anna, Anna!" shouted Mimi. "Are you going to stay here tonight? Say yes."

"I'm staying at Lulu's tonight," said Anna.

"Me, too," added Pam.

Pam and Anna smiled at Lulu. It was the first Lulu had heard about the sleepover. But she still thought it was a perfect idea.

"We're having a Pony Pal sleepover at my house," said Lulu.

Mimi stood on the couch and leaned on her father's head. "Daddy's going to read me four stories tonight," she announced.

"Three," said her father. "That was the deal."

"Thank you girls so much for taking care of Tongo," Mrs. Kline said. "I'm sorry he ran away like that."

"Anna's the only one who took care of him," said Lulu. "I had to take care of Snow White because she was sick."

"And I was at a jumping clinic," added Pam.

Mimi jumped from the couch to the floor. "I can jump," she said. "I'm a great jumper. So is Tongo. He jumped the fence."

The Pony Pals exchanged a glance. This was the perfect time to talk about the fence.

"Maybe that fence should be higher," said Anna. "So Tongo can't jump it."

"If it were a foot higher," suggested Pam, "that would keep him in."

"Having a pony certainly does create problems," said Mrs. Kline with a sigh.

"I suppose we could make it higher," said Mr. Kline. "We have plenty of fence rails in the lumber yard. I could send one of the men over to do it tomorrow."

"That'd be great!" said Pam.

"But what about tonight?" asked Mrs. Kline. "I'm afraid Tongo will jump out." She looked at Anna. "Can Acorn stay here again tonight, Anna?"

"Okay," agreed Anna. "But Acorn has to go home tomorrow." She smiled at Lulu. "Snow White misses him. They're stablemates."

"The fence will be up tomorrow," Mr. Kline said.

"I certainly hope this is the end of our problems with Tongo," added Mrs. Kline.

The Pony Pals exchanged another glance. This was not a good time to ask the Klines to get another animal.

"I'd better check on Tongo and Acorn," said Anna.

"I'll go with you," said Lulu.

"I want to go, too," added Mimi. She ran over to Anna and grabbed her hand.

"And then to bed, young lady," Mimi's father reminded her.

"And then four stories," said Mimi.

"*Three* stories!" said Mr. and Mrs. Kline and Anna in unison.

Everyone laughed.

Lulu and Pam followed Anna and Mimi into the backyard. Tongo nickered when he saw them coming. And Acorn ran over to meet them. He pushed Lulu playfully with his nose.

Lulu scratched his head through his bushy mane. "Acorn!" she said happily. "I miss you. Snow White does, too."

The Pony Pals said good night to Mimi, Acorn

and Tongo. Then they went across the town green to the Harleys' backyard.

Anna held out an apple for Snow White. Snow White grabbed it with her mouth and ate it in three quick chews.

"She's feeling a lot better," laughed Lulu.

After the Pony Pals said good night to Snow White, they went to Lulu's.

Grandmother Sanders was in the living room watching television. "I'm glad you young ladies will be sleeping in a house tonight instead of a barn," she said.

Lulu gave her grandmother a quick hug good night.

The three girls went up to Lulu's room and sat on the bed.

"We didn't tell the Klines about getting another animal," said Pam.

"I was afraid they'd say no," admitted Anna.

"Me, too," agreed Lulu. "So when are we going to ask them?"

"Let's check out the animals at the shelter first," suggested Pam.

"Good idea," said Anna. "We'll go to the animal shelter first thing tomorrow."

"I hope they have a lot of different animals," said Pam.

"Hey, Anna," said Lulu.

When Anna looked up, Lulu threw a pillow at her.

Pam hit Lulu on the head with another pillow. And Anna grabbed Lulu by both wrists while Pam tickled her.

The Pony Pals had a pillow-tickle fight until they were all exhausted.

After Pam and Anna fell asleep, Lulu looked out the window to check on Snow White. Her beautiful white pony was standing alone in the middle of the paddock.

Lulu went downstairs, pulled on her boots and went out into the night. When she reached the paddock, Snow White looked up and walked over to her. Lulu rubbed her hand along Snow

White's side. "Acorn's coming home tomorrow," she said.

Snow White nodded as if she understood. Lulu gave her pony a kiss on the cheek and said good night.

She was happy that Acorn and Snow White would be re-united. But will we find a good stablemate for Tongo, she wondered?

Quack Quack

The next morning the Pony Pals had breakfast at the diner. From the diner they walked on a short-cut trail to Crosshill Road. They walked a half-mile farther and reached St. Francis Animal Shelter. The three girls went into the building to look for the director, Ms. Raskins.

Ms. Raskins was at her desk in the office. Lulu knocked on the open door. Ms. Raskins looked up and smiled. "Hi," she said. "It's nice to see you girls. How did that kitten work out for your friends?"

"Chicago's great," said Anna. "Mimi and Rosalie love him. And he loves them."

"But Chicago's not a stablemate for their pony," explained Lulu. "We came to see what other animals you have."

"We have a lot of different animals right now," said Ms. Raskins. "A cute, pot-bellied pig came to us yesterday. She's in with the goats."

"I didn't even think of a pig for Tongo," Anna whispered to Lulu. "That would be so cute."

The Pony Pals went back outside to see the animals.

Anna pointed to three ducks waddling around the yard. "I love ducks," she said. "They're fun to draw."

One of the ducks quacked and waddled over to Anna. Anna took a few steps to the right. The duck moved to the right. Anna moved to the left. The duck followed her again. Then the duck raised its head in the air and quacked like crazy.

"That one is really cute," said Pam. "Mimi would love it."

"Maybe Tongo would, too," said Lulu. She took out her notebook and wrote:

Duck with brown tips on wings.

"Let's go out the back and see the dogs," suggested Pam.

There were two dogs and two puppies in the dog run behind the building. Ms. Raskins was there, too.

"Did you see the ducks?" she asked.

"They are so cute," said Anna. "One of them came right up to us and quacked."

"That would be Crackers," explained Ms. Raskins. "Those other ducks are afraid of people, but Crackers loves them. She'd follow me around all day if I let her."

"Crackers the Quacker," said Anna with a giggle.

Ms. Raskins opened the gate to the dog run. "Come on in and meet the dogs," she said.

Lulu followed Pam and Anna into the dog run.

A big German Shepherd ran over and jumped excitedly on Lulu. Tongo wouldn't like a dog jumping on him, she thought.

"That's Rufus," said Ms. Raskins.

Pam picked up two fluffy, black puppies. "These guys are so cute," she said.

Lulu bent over the puppies to get a closer look. One of the puppies licked her hand. The other one whimpered as if to say, "Take me home."

"These little fellows were abandoned," Ms. Raskins told the Pony Pals. "I'd love to find a good home for them. I'm hoping to keep them together."

The Klines already have their hands full with Tongo, thought Lulu. They wouldn't want to train even one puppy.

Lulu noticed a small, brown dog with big,

floppy ears and short legs. He was sitting in a corner watching all the excitement.

"What's that dog's name?" Lulu asked Ms. Raskins.

"Oh, that's our wonderful Max," said Ms. Raskins. "We got him last week."

"He seems shy," said Pam.

"Come here, Max," Ms. Raskins called.

Max ran over to Ms. Raskins, sat in front of her and looked up. "Good dog," she said as she bent over and patted him.

"Max is well-trained," Ms. Raskins said. "His owner died recently. That's why he's here. Poor Max. He misses his mistress."

"That's so sad," said Anna.

Lulu took out her notebook and wrote:

Max — sweet dog, small, well-trained.

"Where are the goats and that pot-bellied pig?" asked Pam.

"In the pen behind the shed," Ms. Raskins

told her. "The pig's name is Dottie. She's pretty amazing. You can go right in the pen. The goats are all friendly—especially the little pygmy goat. His name is Billy."

The girls walked over to the shed.

Lulu noticed the three goats first. Two were gray and almost as big as Tongo. The third one was light brown and much smaller.

Lulu heard the pig's little grunting noises before they saw her.

"There's Dottie," Pam said. "Near the shed."

A round, pink head peeked from behind a tree stump.

"Let's go and see her," said Lulu as she opened the gate.

Dottie rolled over, oinked and followed the Pony Pals around the goat yard.

"Dottie's great," said Pam. "It would be so much fun if Tongo had a pig."

"She gets along fine with goats," said Lulu. "So she'd probably get along with a pony."

Billy the goat walked up to Lulu and he

lowered his head. She thought he was going to butt her. But he didn't.

She scratched his head. "You are so friendly, Billy," she said. "And not rough."

Lulu took out her notebook and added two animals to her list.

Dottie the pig and Billy Goat.

"Which animal do you think would make the best stablemate for Tongo?" Pam asked Lulu.

"Maybe Billy," answered Lulu. "I really like him."

"I think Dottie would be the best," said Anna.

"I thought we should try Max," put in Pam.

"I wonder which one Tongo would choose?" asked Lulu.

"It might not be the same one we would pick," said Pam.

"We don't even agree on which one," pointed out Anna.

"I have an idea," said Lulu. "Let's bring Tongo

here. We can introduce him to the animals we liked. That way he can pick for himself."

"We should do that before we tell the Klines our idea about a stablemate," added Anna.

"Good idea," said Pam. She opened the gate and walked out of the pen.

"I hope Tongo likes Dottie best," said Anna as she followed Pam out.

Lulu walked through the gate last and closed it behind her. Which animal will Tongo choose, she wondered?

Tongo's Choice

The Klines' truck was parked in their driveway. Lulu heard the tap-tap of a hammer coming from the backyard.

"They're building the new fence," said Anna.

"Mimi and Tongo are probably in the way," said Pam. "It's a good time to take them to the shelter."

"I have to check on Snow White before I go back to the shelter," Lulu told Pam and Anna.

Pam and Anna went to the Klines' and Lulu went to see Snow White.

As Lulu came through the paddock gate she called to her pony. Snow White looked up and trotted over to her. Lulu rubbed her neck.

Suddenly, Snow White raised her head and whinnied excitedly. Lulu turned around. Anna was leading Acorn down the driveway.

Snow White ran to the gate to meet Acorn, and the two ponies sniffed noses. Acorn nickered as if to say, "I missed you."

"Mrs. Kline is glad that we're taking Tongo and Mimi over to the animal shelter," Anna told Lulu. "Rosalie's coming, too."

"Does Mrs. Kline know that Tongo is picking out a stablemate?" asked Lulu.

"Not yet," said Anna.

The two friends watched their ponies chase each other along the fence line. Snow White kept looking back to be sure her friend was still there.

"I hope Acorn can always stay home now," said Lulu.

"He can if we find Tongo a stablemate," said Anna.

"And if the Klines will take another animal," added Lulu.

"And that's a *big* if," the two friends said together.

Anna and Lulu laughed because they said the same thing at the same time. We're back to being friends like we used to be, thought Lulu. And so are Acorn and Snow White.

Half an hour later the Pony Pals were leading Tongo, Rosalie and Mimi along a short-cut trail through the woods to Crosshill Road.

"We're going to see a lot of different animals," Anna told the girls.

"Don't be too noisy around them," warned Pam. "Some of the animals might be shy."

"Tongo's not shy," said Mimi.

"He certainly isn't," laughed Anna.

When they reached St. Francis Animal Shelter, Tongo sniffed the air curiously.

"He's picking up all the different animal smells," said Pam.

"Let's go and look at the ducks first," suggested Anna.

"I see them!" exclaimed Mimi. She was ready to charge over to the ducks. Anna held her back.

"Let's see what Tongo thinks of them first," suggested Anna.

Lulu led Tongo towards the ducks. Two of them flapped their wings and waddled away quickly. But Crackers ran towards him. The friendly duck was waddling, flapping and quacking all at once.

Tongo took a few steps back and pawed the ground nervously.

Crackers flapped his wings again and jumped towards Tongo's face.

"He's just being friendly," Lulu told Tongo.

Mimi and Rosalie thought Crackers was great fun. They ran around the yard with the duck quacking behind them.

Tongo pulled on the lead to get away from the excited duck. He didn't like that kind of friendly.

Lulu and Anna exchanged a glance. Crackers and Tongo would not be good stablemates.

"Let's try Max next," suggested Pam.

"I'll play with Rufus, so he doesn't jump on the girls," Pam told Lulu. "He might scare them."

When Pam went into the dog run, Rufus ran right over to her. Anna showed Rosalie and Mimi the black puppies. Meanwhile, Lulu led Tongo over to Max.

"Hi, Max," Lulu said in a friendly voice. "I brought you a friend."

Tongo lowered his head and sniffed. He was curious about the little dog. But Max wasn't curious about Tongo. He whimpered fearfully and ran back into the shelter.

"Max doesn't like ponies," Lulu told Pam.

"The puppies are so cute!" exclaimed Rosalie.

"There are two of them," said Mimi excitedly. "I could have one and Rosalie could have one."

"We're looking for one animal for Tongo,"

explained Anna. "You already have Tongo and Chicago."

"Okay," said Mimi.

Lulu led Tongo out of the dog run. Ms. Raskins was waiting for them.

"Look at that cute pony," she said. "Has he met Dottie yet?"

"That's where we're going next," said Lulu. "I hope she likes him. Max was afraid."

"Dottie might be shy at first," said Ms. Raskins. "But she'll get over it. Remember that you can always try an animal out. If it doesn't fit in, we'll take him or her back."

"Thanks," said Lulu.

Tongo and Lulu led the way to the goat pen. Pam opened the gate and they all went in.

Dottie was lying in the mud near the tree stump. The goats were in the shed. Tongo pulled on the lead to go closer to her. Billy Goat noticed Tongo and followed him over to Dottie.

Lulu and Pam exchanged a smile. Dottie wasn't running away.

Tongo sniffed the little pig. He wrinkled his nose and nickered as if to say, "I don't like that smell."

Dottie walked back to her tree stump and Tongo turned away.

"That pig is so cute," said Rosalie. "But I don't think Tongo likes her."

"She doesn't like Tongo, either," added Mimi.

Just then, Tongo noticed Billy Goat beside him. Tongo nickered a hello and dropped his head to sniff the goat.

Billy put his head in butting position. Pam went to grab him before he butted Tongo. But Lulu put out a hand to stop her. "Wait," Lulu whispered.

Tongo nuzzled the top of Billy's head.

"What are they doing?" asked Rosalie.

"Making friends," answered Lulu.

"I guess we found a stablemate for Tongo," said Pam.

"I hope the Klines will adopt him," said Anna.

I hope so, too, thought Lulu.

Bad Timing

Tongo and Billy Goat walked around the pen together. Ms. Raskins came up to the fence to watch them. "Those two are getting along nicely," she said. "A goat makes a great stablemate for a pony."

"Can I have Billy?" begged Mimi.

"It would be lovely if you could give him a good home," said Ms. Raskins.

"Yeah!" shouted Mimi. "I want Billy to come home with me now."

"You can't just take a goat home," Lulu told Mimi.

"We have to ask your parents," added Anna.

A few minutes later the girls and Tongo left the shelter. Mimi ran ahead on the trail.

"Hurry up, everybody!" she shouted. "We have to tell Mommy about Billy."

"Mimi could ruin everything," Anna whispered to Lulu.

"With bad timing?" asked Lulu.

Anna nodded.

"Mimi!" Lulu called. "Come back here. We have to tell you something."

Mimi ran back to the Pony Pals and walked between Anna and Lulu. Pam and Rosalie followed with Tongo.

"Don't tell your mom about Billy as soon as you get home," warned Lulu.

"Your parents might not want another animal," added Pam.

"But I want Billy," whined Mimi.

"There's a good time and a bad time to ask

for a big favor from parents," added Pam. "Getting a new pet is a very big favor. Especially when you have two already."

"I know," said Mimi.

"Let us ask her for you," suggested Anna. "We'll know the best time to do it."

"Okay," agreed Mimi.

When the girls reached the Klines', they led Tongo around to the backyard. Mrs. Kline and a carpenter were still working on the new fence.

Mrs. Kline met them at the gate. Lulu noticed that she looked very tired.

"This fence is a lot of trouble," Mrs. Kline said.

"Mommy! Mommy!" said Mimi excitedly. "I want Billy. I have to have him. Tongo wants him, too."

"Billy who?" asked Mrs. Kline.

"Billy's a goat," explained Rosalie. "He can be Tongo's stablemate. Then Tongo won't run away again."

"I thought that's why we've been building a

new fence," said Mrs. Kline. She shot an angry look at the Pony Pals. "So what's this about a goat?"

The cell phone on Mrs. Kline's belt rang. She turned from the girls to answer it.

The Pony Pals exchanged a quick glance. They needed three ideas. And fast.

"Mimi," said Anna in a low voice. "Your mom is tired. Let's go and get her some lemonade."

Anna took Mimi by the hand and led her towards the house.

"Can I help?" asked Rosalie.

"You can help me put Tongo in the shed," Pam told her.

Pam handed Rosalie Tongo's lead rope and they headed to the shed. Lulu looked around to see what she could do to help. The yard looked messy. I'll do some cleaning up, she decided.

Mrs. Kline was on the phone for a long time. When she finished the call, the carpenter went over to her.

"We've finally finished the fence," he said.

"Thank you, Ralph," said Mrs. Kline.

Ralph waved to Lulu. "Thanks for helping with the clean-up," he said.

Lulu looked around at the fence. It looked great. The clean-up was almost finished. And Tongo was in his shed happily munching on hay.

Anna and Mimi came out of the house with a pitcher of lemonade, a stack of glasses and a plate of cookies.

"Mommy, I made you some lemonade!" shouted Mimi.

A few minutes later the five girls and Mrs. Kline were sitting around the picnic table having a snack.

"This is the first time I've sat down all day," Mrs. Kline said. She looked around the yard. "But the fence looks good." She smiled at the Pony Pals. "It's an improvement."

"And Tongo can't jump over it," said Pam.

Mrs. Kline's smile turned to a frown. "But what's this about a goat?" she asked.

"I want him," said Mimi. "Tongo does, too."

"We saw a goat at the animal shelter," explained Lulu.

"He's a very sweet goat," said Anna. "He got along great with Tongo."

"They made friends right away," added Pam. "He'd make a great stablemate for Tongo."

Mrs. Kline sighed. "We have so much to do taking care of Tongo," she said.

"We have a goat," Pam told Mrs. Kline. "They're not a lot of trouble."

"We'll help," said Anna.

"Me, too," added Rosalie.

Mrs. Kline patted Rosalie's hand. "You are a great help with Tongo," she said. "And Chicago."

"I love animals," said Rosalie.

"Me, too!" exclaimed Mimi. "I love animals."

Lulu poured Mrs. Kline another glass of lemonade. "It isn't a very big goat," she said.

"Please, Mommy, please," begged Mimi.

"I'll have to talk to your father about it," said Mrs. Kline. "And I want to meet this wonderful goat."

"Call Daddy now!" pleaded Mimi. *Please*."

"I guess I could," said Mrs. Kline as she opened her cell phone. She stood up and went to the other end of the yard to call her husband.

The five girls waited. Lulu crossed her fingers and hoped that Mrs. Kline would let Tongo have Billy Goat for a stablemate.

Traffic Jam

Mimi's mother talked on her cell phone for a long time. Lulu wished that she could hear what she was saying. Finally Mrs. Kline came back to the picnic table.

"Did Daddy say yes?" asked Mimi. "Did he? Did he?"

"He did," Mrs. Kline said. "But—"

"Yeah!" shouted Mimi.

"But," Mrs. Kline repeated, "the goat can't stay unless he's a perfect stablemate for

Tongo. If there is any trouble, we are *not* keeping him."

"Can we go get him now?" begged Mimi. "Please!"

"Tomorrow will be soon enough," said Mrs. Kline. "I'll call the animal shelter and make the arrangements."

The Pony Pals exchanged a smile. Their plan was working perfectly.

The next morning the Pony Pals went to the Klines'. Mimi and Rosalie met them in the front yard.

"How does Tongo like his new fence?" asked Lulu.

"He didn't run away last night," said Mimi.

"That's because he can't get over the fence," said Rosalie. "He's still lonely. I can tell."

"Come see what we made," said Mimi. "Hurry!"

The Pony Pals followed Mimi to the backyard. A big paper sign hung on the shed.

TONGO AND BILLY GOAT LIVE HERE!

"Rosalie wrote the words," explained Mimi.

"It's a nice sign," said Anna.

"But don't forget," added Lulu, "Billy might not be able to stay."

"I know," said Mimi sadly.

Lulu heard a car and horse trailer pull in the driveway.

"He's here!" shouted Rosalie.

The five girls ran over to the trailer. Tongo whinnied as if to say, "What's going on?"

Mrs. Kline came out of the house to greet Ms. Raskins and meet Billy. Everyone stood near the trailer door while Ms. Raskins opened it.

Lulu looked inside the trailer and saw the small goat standing in the corner. Pam put down the ramp.

"Come on, Billy," Anna called.

Billy walked slowly to the edge of the ramp. He looked around at the crowd waiting for him.

"It's okay, Billy," Ms. Raskins said. "This is your new home."

"Might be your new home," corrected Mrs. Kline.

Suddenly, Billy ran down the ramp, pushed Rosalie over and charged down the driveway towards the street.

"Catch him," shouted Pam.

"Billy! Billy!" called Mimi.

"Grab him by the collar!" yelled Ms. Raskins.

Lulu ran after Billy. He made a right turn

onto the front lawn, but he was too fast for Lulu. Ms. Raskins, Pam and Anna were trying to catch him, too.

Billy ran and leapt across the lawn onto the sidewalk. Main Street was busy with passing cars and trucks. I have to catch Billy before he goes on the road, thought Lulu.

Billy kicked up his back heels and ran to the road. He thought it was all a game.

"Get him from the front," Lulu shouted to Pam.

Pam ran into the street and grabbed Billy by the collar.

A car screeched to a halt in front of them. "Hey, what's going on?" yelled the driver of the car.

"Sorry," Lulu called to him.

"Well, get that goat out of the way!" the driver shouted.

The driver in a pickup truck behind the car honked his horn.

Pam pulled on Billy from the front. Lulu pushed from behind, but he wouldn't budge.

"So this is Billy," Lulu heard Mrs. Kline say to Ms. Raskins. "I thought he wasn't going to be any trouble."

Pam and Lulu exchanged a glance. So far, Billy was not making a great impression.

"Let's carry him," Lulu told Pam. "I'll take the front."

Lulu put her arms under the front of Billy's belly and Pam took the back.

"I was just going to suggest that," Ms. Raskins said.

Billy grabbed Lulu's sleeve with his teeth and yanked. "Hey," said Lulu. "Let go!"

Mimi ran up to them. "He's so funny," shouted Mimi. "Isn't he funny?"

"Mimi!" shouted Mrs. Kline. "Out of the road!"

"Let's carry him to the yard," suggested Lulu.

"I'll open the gate," said Anna. "Rosalie and Mimi, you come with me."

Pam and Lulu carried Billy into the yard.

Everyone followed them in. Tongo whinnied a hello and took a few steps towards Billy.

When the gate was closed, Pam and Lulu put Billy down. The goat took one look at Tongo and ran in the other direction.

"I thought you said Tongo and Billy liked one another," said Mrs. Kline.

Lulu looked around the yard. Today he's been in a horse trailer, she thought. Then he ran into traffic. Now he's in a strange, small yard with seven people and a pony. That's a lot for one little goat to go through.

"Let's leave Tongo and Billy alone for a little while," suggested Lulu. "So they can get used to one another."

"I'll give him some water and food," said Pam. "That will calm him down."

"I think that's a splendid idea," said Ms. Raskins. "I have to go back to the animal shelter." She smiled at Mrs. Kline. "Call me if he doesn't work out. I'll come right back and take him."

Billy stuck his head between the fence rails and ate a rose.

"No, Billy," yelled Mrs. Kline. She turned to Ms. Raskins. "It doesn't look like it's going to work out," said Mrs. Kline. "Maybe you should just take him back now."

"No, Mommy, no!" shouted Mimi.

"Sh-hh," Anna told Mimi. "You'll scare Billy with all of your shouting."

Mimi took Anna's hand. "Sorry," she said.

"I'll call you later," Mrs. Kline told Ms. Raskins.

Ms. Raskins left and everyone but Pam and Lulu went into the house.

Billy ran in different directions around the yard. Once he stopped to sniff a pile of pony plop. Tongo stood perfectly still and watched everything that Billy did.

"Do you think Tongo is afraid of him?" Lulu asked Pam.

"No," said Pam. "But he's not sure if he likes him either."

Lulu and Pam moved slowly and quietly around the paddock. Lulu gave Tongo a handful of grain while Pam fed Billy. Billy stopped running around when he saw the food. He gobbled it up. When he was finished, he looked across the yard to see what Tongo was doing.

Tongo chewed and watched Billy. And Billy watched Tongo. Suddenly, Tongo gave a soft, sweet-sounding nicker.

Billy's ears went forward. He made a throaty noise.

Tongo took a few steps forward. This time Billy didn't run away. Tongo took a few more steps. Billy ran up to Tongo. The two animals sniffed each other's faces like best animal friends.

Lulu noticed Mrs. Kline, Anna and the younger girls watching from the kitchen window. They were all smiling, even Mrs. Kline.

Lulu and Pam met at the gate. "Let's leave them alone for awhile," said Pam.

"Good idea," said Lulu. She looked at her

watch. It was only eleven o'clock. "And let's go on a trail ride this afternoon. Just the Pony Pals."

"Perfect," said Pam. "I'll go in and get Anna."

"I'll meet you in Acorn and Snow White's paddock," said Lulu. She ran towards the town green. She couldn't wait to see her own pony with her stablemate.

Lulu stopped at the fence to watch Snow White and Acorn grazing side by side.

The Pony Pals are going for a trail ride, thought Lulu. Three girls and their ponies . . . everything is back to normal.

Dear Pony Pal:

There are now Pony Pals all over the United States, Australia, New Zealand, Canada, Germany and Norway.

When I first started writing the Pony Pals I thought there would only be six books. Now there are twenty-six books. I am surprised that I have so many stories to tell about Pam, Anna, Lulu and their ponies. They are like real people, who keep having adventures that I want to write down for them.

When I am not writing Pony Pal or CHEER USA books, I like to swim, hike, draw and paint. I also like to visit horse farms and talk to people who love and ride ponies and horses. I don't ride anymore and have never owned my own pony or horse. But my husband and I have two young cats, Lucca and Todi. They are brothers and get along great with our old dog, Willie.

It's wonderful to know that so many Pony Pals from different parts of the world enjoy the adventures of Pam, Anna, Lulu, Lightning, Acorn and Snow White. I think about you when I am writing. A special thankyou to those who have written me letters and sent drawings and photos. I love your drawings of ponies and keep your photos on the wall near my computer. They inspire me to write more Pony Pal stories.

Remember, you don't need a pony to be a Pony Pal.

Happy Reading,

Jeanne Betancourt